D1219085

GRAPHIC MYTHICAL CREATURES

TROLLS

BY GARY JEFFREY
ILLUSTRATED BY JAMES FIELD

Gareth Stevens
Publishing

Please visit our website, www.garethstevens.com.
For a free color catalog of all our high-quality books,
call toll free 1-800-542-2595 or fax 1-877-542-2596.

Library of Congress Cataloging-in-Publication Data

Jeffrey, Gary.
Trolls / Gary Jeffrey.
p. cm. — (Graphic mythical creatures)
Includes index.
ISBN 978-1-4339-6047-5 (pbk.)
ISBN 978-1-4339-6048-2 (6-pack)
ISBN 978-1-4339-6045-1 (library binding)
1. Trolls. I. Title.
GR555.J44 2012
398.2—dc22
2011003040

First Edition

Published in 2012 by
Gareth Stevens Publishing
111 East 14th Street, Suite 349
New York, NY 10003

Designed by David West Books
Editor: Ronne Randall

Photo credits:
p4, DannyWS

Printed in China

CPSIA compliance information: Batch #DS11GS: For further information contact Gareth Stevens, New York, New York at 1-800-542-2595.

CONTENTS

TROLL TALES

Big-nosed, hairy, and smelly, the troll is always an evil character in the mythology of northern lands. The trolls of folklore can vary greatly in shape and size but are almost always extremely mean spirited.

A hideous troll lurks under a bridge, ready to surprise the unwary.

This statue has all the typical features of a troll.

Scandinavian trolls were often giants.

TROLL TRUTHS

There are many tales of trolls guarding bridges or forests for no other reason than to keep people away. Trolls can live inside mountains and can even lurk in lakes! Some trolls are able to shape-shift at will—a dangerous power. However, trolls are usually undone by their slowness and their stupidity. Traditionally, trolls are afraid of sunlight.

Troll Types

Mountain trolls are treasure hoarders, while forest trolls like to arm themselves with clubs. Trolls can have multiple heads or just a single eye! Lowland trolls also have a cow's tail. Trolls are said to stir their porridge with their long noses. Outgrowths of trees and bushes can enable a hill troll to blend with its surroundings.

A bizarre, multiheaded mountain troll from a Swedish fairy tale. Trolls can have up to nine heads!

This huge troll has disguised himself as a hill, complete with trees.

Troll Lore

Interest in trolls continues to this day. Oddly shaped rocks in Scandinavia are said to be trolls that were turned to stone when caught by the first rays of the sun.

A troll stone in Norway

THE TROLLS OF HEDALE WOODS

SOMETHING...
SNUFFLING!
THE SOUND WAS UNMISTAKABLE - THE LOUD SNIFFING OF...

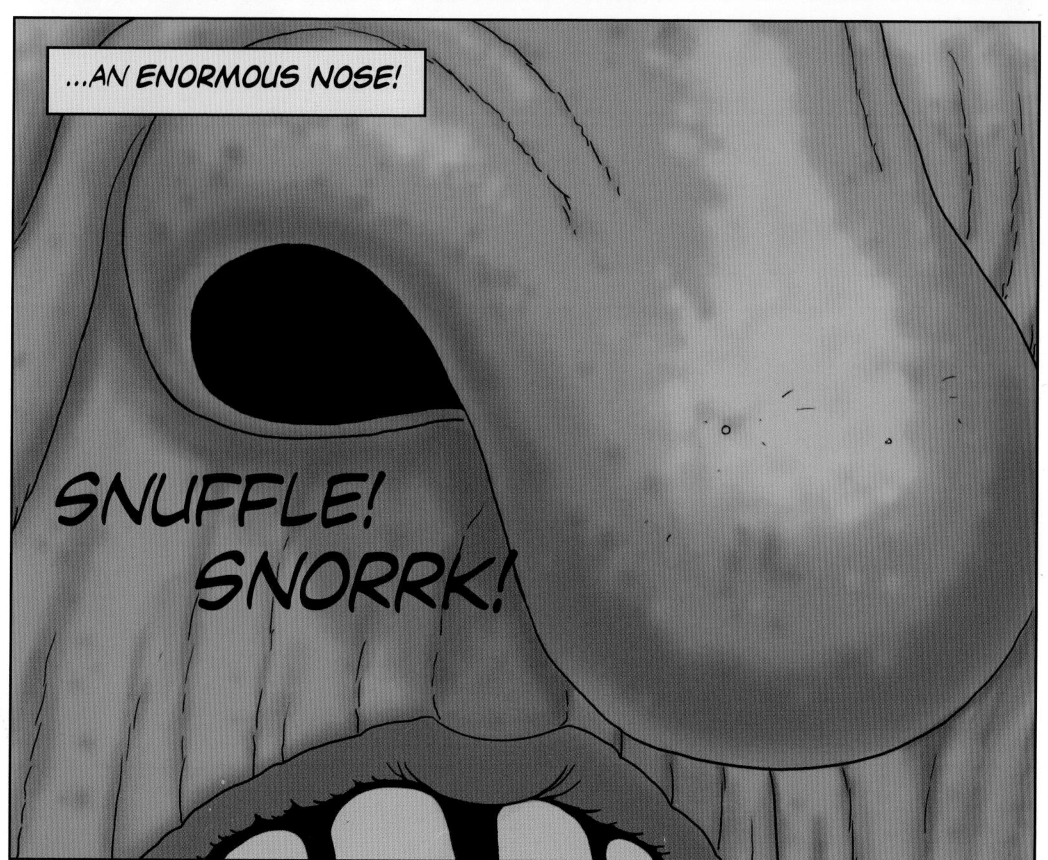
...AN ENORMOUS NOSE!
SNUFFLE!
SNORRK!

THE NOSE ROSE HIGH
ABOVE THE TREETOPS.
I SMELL HUMAN
BLOOD HERE!

OH, NO! IT'S A
TROLL! WHAT
DO WE DO?

YOU GRAB THE BAGS AND GET READY TO RUN.
I'M GOING TO HIDE IN THE TREES...

...WITH MY **AX.**

A TROLL BURST THROUGH THE TREES, CLOSELY FOLLOWED BY TWO MORE.
YIKES! THEY'VE SPOTTED ME!

FROM HIS HIDING PLACE, THE OLDER BROTHER LOOKED UP...
THE FRONT ONE IS LEADING THEM. THE OTHERS ARE BLIND!

THE TROLLS ONLY HAD ONE EYE AMONG THEM, WHICH THEY HAD TO SHARE.

THEY ADVANCED ON THE YOUNGER BOY, WHO HAD STARTED TO RUN.
THERE THEY GO...

THE OLDER BROTHER CREPT UP TO THE TROLL'S ANKLE, DREW BACK HIS AX, AND...

THUNK!
YEEEOWW!

WHAT WAS THAT?
THE EYE!

GOT IT!
IT WAS AS BIG AS A COOKING POT.

HE LOOKED THROUGH THE EYE.
IT'S AMAZING - EVERYTHING'S AS CLEAR AS DAY!
GIVE IT BACK!

GIVE IT BACK, OR WE'LL TURN YOU TO **STONE!**
I'D LIKE TO SEE YOU TRY WITHOUT AN EYE!

GIVE IT BACK, YOU LITTLE WASP, OR WE'LL-
NOT SO FAST OR I'LL COME OVER THERE AND CUT THE REST OF YOUR ANKLES! YOU'LL HAVE TO CRAWL HOME LIKE CRABS!

THE TROLLS WHISPERED AMONG THEMSELVES FOR A MINUTE.

ALL RIGHT, WE'LL GIVE YOU GOLD AND SILVER AND ANYTHING ELSE YOU WANT FOR THE EYE.
VERY GOOD, BUT I MUST HAVE THE TREASURE FIRST, OR NO EYE.

THE TROLLS PLEADED.
IF YOU'LL JUST LEND IT TO US FOR A MOMENT!
BUT HOW CAN WE GET IT IF WE CAN'T SEE?
NO WAY!

ONE OF THE TROLLS HAD AN IDEA AND SHOUTED AS LOUD AS HE COULD TOWARD A FAR HILL.
?!
MOTHER! WE NEED GOLD AND SILVER TO TRADE FOR OUR EYE!

SOON AN OLD LADY CAME LUMBERING TOWARD THEM WITH BUCKETS OF TREASURE.

SHE WAS NOT VERY PLEASED.
HOW **DARE** YOU BLACKMAIL MY SONS BY **TAKING** THEIR **EYE**!

MOTHER, DON'T SPEAK TOO **HARSHLY**, OR THE LITTLE WASP MAY TAKE YOUR EYE TOO!

THE OLD WOMAN THREW DOWN THE BUCKETS.
CHINK
BOK!

THE LEAD TROLL SCREWED HIS EYE BACK INTO PLACE.
COME ON, BOYS, LET'S GET AWAY FROM THESE EVIL CREATURES!

THAT'S RIGHT, AWAY WITH YOU! AND DON'T GO SNIFFING FOR HUMAN BLOOD IN HEDALE WOODS ANYMORE!
...AND THEY NEVER DID.
THE END

Other Famous Troll Stories

The long, cold northern winters of long ago have left us a rich collection of folk stories. All legends need heroes and villains. Along with his cousin the ogre, the troll reigns in this fairy tale world as bad guy supreme…

The Three Billy Goats Gruff
The famous Norwegian fairy tale of the three goats who use their wits to overcome a troll who is guarding a bridge.

The Troll with No Heart in His Body
An epic folktale telling how a young prince rescues his six brothers and a fair princess who are imprisoned at a troll's castle. With the help of a talking wolf, a raven, and a salmon, he finds the troll's heart and destroys it.

Askeladden is surprised by a troll in the woods.

The Sailors and the Troll
A lovesick troll tries to trick some Norwegian sailors into helping him kidnap a maiden who has rejected his proposal of marriage.

Outrunning a Hulder
A hulder is a female troll disguised as a woman. In this story, a hulder tries to trick a farm boy into marriage. He escapes using her special brass skis.

Askeladden and the Troll
The son of a poor farmer defeats a troll and gains his treasure by tricking him in an eating contest.

GLOSSARY

bizarre Odd, unusual, and not what one would expect.

blackmail To obtain something from someone by taking something valuable from them or through the use of threats.

epic A long narrative poem that tells the dramatic story of a legendary hero.

folklore Traditional beliefs, myths, and tales that are passed down through generations by word of mouth.

hoarder Someone who keeps a hidden supply of something, usually treasure or food, for future use.

lurk To lie in wait, unobserved, often for evil purposes.

mythology A collection of myths or stories about a people which tells of their origin, history, ancestors, and heroes.

plead To appeal very seriously or beg, usually so that someone changes their mind or decision.

shape-shift To alter one's physical appearance, usually in order to trick someone.

unwary Not alert to danger or deception.

wits Intelligence and the ability to reason and act quickly.

yore A time that is long past.

Index